Might goes hand in hand with right as He-Man and the Masters of the Universe fight to make their planet safe. The greatest of their enemies is Skeletor, the Lord of Destruction, and his evil band, whose hatred for their foes is never-ending. The war goes on but who will win?

British Library Cataloguing in Publication Data

Grant, John, *1930-*
    He-Man meets the beast. —(Masters of the universe; 6)
    I. Title   II. Davies, Robin, *1950-*   III. Series
    823'.914[J]   PZ7
    ISBN 0-7214-0906-7

First edition

© LADYBIRD BOOKS LTD MCMLXXXV and MATTEL INC MCMLXXXV

MASTERS
OF THE UNIVERSE™

He-Man meets the Beast

by John Grant
illustrated by Robin Davies

Ladybird Books Loughborough

The people of Eternia were celebrating their king's birthday. Since early morning they had been arriving at the royal palace with gifts. Flags fluttered from every tower. To the sound of music the people strolled in the royal gardens where tables were set out with food and drink. And in the great hall of the palace the king and his family entertained the nobility of Eternia to a great banquet.

When the tables had been cleared it was the turn of the king's jester Orko. The guests roared with laughter as the strange little alien performed his magic tricks. Most of them went wrong, but that was part of the entertainment.

Far away in Snake Mountain, Skeletor, Lord of Destruction, and his wicked accomplice, Evil-Lyn, watched the celebrations on a video spy-scan monitor. They saw Orko finish his act, then heard the king call for silence.

"It is my plan," he said, "to set off soon on a tour of my kingdom. I shall take Prince Adam and Teela along with me. It is time that they met the people of Eternia."

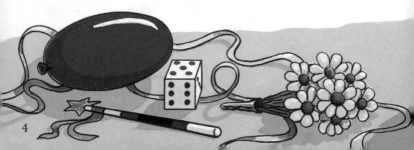

Angrily Skeletor switched off the monitor.

"That weakling does not deserve the name of 'king'," he cried. "Those creatures bringing him gifts! Laughing! Singing! They should tremble at his word! They should fear his very look! Such happiness and contentment sickens me!"

At that moment one of Skeletor's slaves came creeping out of the shadows of Snake Mountain. "O Great One," he said, bowing low, "I have heard that King Randor plans to travel by way of the Plain of Perpetua. Does the news please Your Lordship?"

It was Evil-Lyn who spoke. "Now is our chance," she said. "Below the plain lies the Labyrinth of Perpetua. Lure one of the royal children into its depths. The beasts of the Labyrinth will soon make an end of them. That will strike a harder blow against the forces of good than all the weapons in Snake Mountain."

Mounting Panthor, Skeletor and Evil-Lyn headed for the Plain of Perpetua. The giant cat's huge stride swiftly covered the distance. At last they saw what they were looking for — a pile of ruins, and in its midst the shattered remains of an archway.

Skeletor pulled Panthor to a halt a short way from the ruins. They could see that the arch had almost totally collapsed. But there was a narrow gap between the tumbled blocks of stone where a person might just squeeze through.

Leaving Evil-Lyn to keep watch outside, Skeletor passed through the opening and into the Labyrinth. He held his Havoc-Staff at the ready. Ever since the great volcanic eruptions of thousands of years ago, all manner of evil monsters had remained trapped below ground. Strange cries echoed out of the depths and eyes shone from the shadows as the Lord of Destruction went deeper and deeper, seeking a particular cavern and its awful inhabitant.

The only light in the Labyrinth came from strange luminous clumps of fungus growing on the rocks and faintly glowing outcrops of crystal. As he felt his way carefully with the Havoc-Staff, Skeletor peered at the rocky walls on either side of the passage. At last he found what he was looking for. Where the rock wall was flat and smooth there were carved letters in the ancient Eternian language.

Stepping back a couple of paces the Lord of Destruction held up the Havoc-Staff and sent a stream of energy playing over the rock. For a moment nothing happened, then the great slab

swung to one side. Beyond was a vast cavern.
And in the centre of the cavern a monstrous
shape lay on the rocky floor... the behemoth,
the most terrible of all the creatures of the
Labyrinth of Perpetua. It had been put into a
deep sleep thousands of years ago by the Council
of Elders.

Stretching out his Staff, Skeletor sent a surge
of power towards the slumbering monster. The
huge body quivered. The eyes opened and
began to glow. And slowly the behemoth heaved
itself to its feet.

Far across the plain, King Randor and his
company approached in their fleet of hover
coaches. Prince Adam and Teela had grown
bored with sitting in a coach, and now they
galloped on either side of the convoy. Teela
rode her golden horse. Adam borrowed a horse
from the Royal Guard. Cringer, the cowardly
Eternian tiger, loped along beside them. On a
level stretch of grassland sheltered by a low
ridge, the royal vehicles swung into a circle and

halted. Within a few moments the king's servants were preparing the camp for the night.

Hidden behind a rocky outcrop, Skeletor and Evil-Lyn watched as the tents and pavilions arose. Then they saw something else. Prince Adam, with nothing else to do, had decided to ride out with Cringer to explore.

"The fool!" cried Skeletor. "He is playing right into our hands!"

Skeletor and Evil-Lyn hurried back to the Labyrinth. While Skeletor retraced his footsteps through the sinister passages, Evil-Lyn went to Panthor. From a saddle bag she lifted out a voice-beam projector, a device which could imitate any voice and make it appear to come from any direction.

Inside the ruined arch Evil-Lyn found a hiding place amongst the tumbled stones. Then she settled down to wait.

Skeletor was now at the entrance to the behemoth's cavern. The monster was still only half awake. It stood unsteadily on its feet, shaking its head slowly from side to side.

Skeletor boosted the Havoc-Staff to full power.

"You have slept long enough!" he cried. "Now is the moment for you to seek revenge against those who imprisoned you!"

The power from the Staff crackled around the behemoth, bathing it in light. Its eyes glowed with fire. Its muscles rippled as it stretched. Then, with an ear-splitting roar it turned towards the entrance to the cavern.

Out on the open plain, Prince Adam halted
for a moment. He looked around. Apart from
occasional masses of tumbled rock there was
nothing to see. But there was one pile of rock
which looked different. He rode closer. It was
the remains of some kind of structure.
Crumbling stone pillars held up a half-broken
arch. The space below the arch was almost
blocked with fallen stone.

The prince urged his horse forward. But
Cringer whimpered, took a few steps, and
stopped. He shook with terror. Even Adam felt
that all was not well, but he dismounted and
approached the arch on foot while Cringer
backed off to a safe distance.

Prince Adam stood in the shadow of the
ancient building and saw a gap in the stones
blocking the entrance. It was just wide enough
for him to squeeze through. A tunnel stretched
ahead of him, faintly lit by glowing fungus and
fragments of radioactive crystal.

Adam could feel evil all about him. He was
about to return through the arch when he heard
a sound.

From far down the tunnel echoed a cry:

"HELP! HELP! COME QUICKLY!"

With not a moment's hesitation Adam ran
down the sloping tunnel. "Hang on!" he cried.
"I'm coming!"

Soon the glimmer of moonlight which marked
the entrance was left far behind. Adam's
footsteps echoed as he ran between jagged
stalagmites and around cracks and crevices in
the rocky floor. And all the time the cries for

help seemed to come from somewhere just around the next bend in the passage. There were other sounds, too. Growls and snarls sounded from shadowy side tunnels, and glowing eyes kept track of the prince's movements.

He realised suddenly that the voice had stopped. Was he too late? What he did not know was that Evil-Lyn, hiding near the entrance, had paused to readjust her voice-beam projector.

Again came the cries for help. But now the voice was unmistakably that of Teela.

At the sound of Teela's voice, Adam paused. How could it be? He had seen her in camp before he set out to explore. She had the swiftest horse in all Eternia, he knew; but she could not have reached the broken arch before him.

But still someone was calling for help. He ran on quickly.

Again the voice was silent. But now the prince could hear something behind him. He listened. There came the sound of heavy footfalls. Then a

distant growling which grew to an ear-splitting roar. Dust and fragments of stone showered down from the roof of the tunnel at the noise. For a moment Adam was deafened. The roaring came again... but much nearer. Now he could hear the heavy breathing of some large creature.

Adam backed into a crevice in the wall of the tunnel. In the distance two huge eyes glowed like fire. In the faint light of the tunnel a terrifying shape cut off his line of retreat.

Adam fled for his life. As he ran he
remembered the old stories. This must be the
Labyrinth of Perpetua. And his pursuer must be
the terrible behemoth. He had seen pictures of
it in books.

In spite of its giant size, the behemoth moved
quickly. Adam was soon panting for breath as
he doubled to and fro through the maze of
tunnels and passages.

In his other role as He-Man, mightiest man in the Universe, the prince had nothing to fear from even so vast an enemy. But without the Power Sword he was only the weak and feckless Adam. As he ran he sent out desperate thought signals to Teela. Perhaps in her role of warrior goddess she might be able to help. But far underground, and with no more strength than an ordinary man, Adam could only try to out-run the monster and find a hiding place.

The tunnel suddenly opened out into a lofty cavern. Stalactites hung from the roof casting black shadows across the rocky floor. Adam dived into the shadows and saw that several passages opened out from the cavern. Still in the shadow of the stalactites he ran noiselessly into the cover of the nearest passage.

The behemoth charged into the cavern. And stopped. It had lost sight of its prey. It turned its head from side to side listening, and Adam

held his breath. Then the monstrous beast
lowered its head to the floor and began to sniff.
It turned this way and that. Then it picked up
the prince's scent. With a roar it turned towards
the tunnel where he was hiding.

Prince Adam didn't wait. He ran even faster
than before.

Ahead there was the sound of falling water.
An underground stream poured over a high rock
in a rushing waterfall before flowing along the
tunnel floor to be lost in the darkness. This
might be Prince Adam's chance. Animals, he
knew, could not follow a scent through flowing

water. Without a moment's hesitation he splashed into the stream. The sound of the water drowned the noise as he waded knee-deep. The behemoth reached the water's edge but Prince Adam was already out of sight around a bend in the stream.

The behemoth screamed with rage when it realised that it had lost its victim. It strained its yellow eyes into the gloom. But there was no sign of the prince.

Adam climbed out of the water and pulled himself up the rocky bank. A loose rock moved under his hand. Then it rolled with an echoing splash into the stream.

In a flash the chase was on again.

Perched safely upon a rocky ledge near the entrance to the Labyrinth, Skeletor listened to the roaring of the behemoth as it echoed and re-echoed from the hidden depths of the maze of passages.

"AT LAST!" he cried in triumph. "THE PRINCE OF ETERNIA IS ABOUT TO MEET HIS DOOM!"

Evil-Lyn hurried to join him. "This will be a sad day indeed for Planet Eternia," she said, smiling. "And I think that it would be most fitting, My Lord of Destruction, if you were to bear the sad tidings to King Randor yourself."

Skeletor threw back his head and roared with evil laughter. "That will be my special pleasure," he cried. "But come. We must be absolutely sure. And we must check all the details of the sad end of His Highness."

And together the Lord of Destruction and his wicked partner hurried into the darkness.

Prince Adam was by now desperate. Nothing it seemed would shake off the terrifying creature. Even where the Labyrinth was blackest he could hear it snuffling at the ground as it followed his scent.

Then in the faint light of an outcrop of radioactive crystal, he saw something that gave him hope. Some distance ahead, a rocky ledge projected from the tunnel wall. It was well above his head.

Prince Adam looked back. The behemoth was coming on fast. But its head was down as it followed his scent. With luck it might not have seen him yet.

The prince sprinted towards the ledge and leapt upwards. His finger-tips just managed to gain a hold. Panting, he hauled himself up.

Then he peered over the edge. The behemoth stopped, puzzled. The scent stopped without warning. It stood for a moment. Then it backed away to wait until its victim reappeared.

Back at the royal camp, Cringer had returned
alone at dawn. The king raged about his missing
son. "Why can't that foolish boy take advice
occasionally? He was told that the Plain of
Perpetua was dangerous. Now he has got
himself lost! Captain of the Guard! Send out a
search party immediately!"

Teela listened to the king. She knew that it
was most unlikely that the prince was lost. He
must be in trouble of some sort. Earlier her
mind had picked up a faint thought signal. It
was a distress call. But from whom and from
where she knew not.

Teela mounted her golden horse and called to Cringer, "Take me to where you left your master!"

Reluctantly Cringer led Teela across the plain. When he came within sight of the ruined entrance to the Labyrinth he whined and refused to go further. Tethering her horse and holding her Kobra power sceptre at the ready, Teela entered the Labyrinth.

Teela had only taken a few steps down the tunnel when her sceptre began to glow. There was danger ahead. The creatures of the Labyrinth, disturbed by Skeletor and Evil-Lyn and then by Adam and the behemoth, were creeping out of their dens.

A giant centipede swarmed down the rock face towards her, but a blast from the sceptre sent it hurrying back. Then came another. And

Teela had only beaten off that attack when a
noise behind made her turn on her heel. A
swarm of hairy, humanoid orcs came scurrying
out of a dark cave mouth. Back to the wall,
Teela sent bolt after bolt into their midst. But
for every one knocked flying another two seemed
to rush out of the shadows.

Teela began a fighting retreat to the entrance.
Alone she could not win through to Prince
Adam. She must seek help.

Teela hurried back to the royal camp. It was almost deserted. Most of the company had gone off in search of the missing prince.

Then she spotted Orko the court jester practising a new conjuring trick. Quickly she told him that Prince Adam was trapped in the Labyrinth of Perpetua. Orko nodded. "Leave it to me," he said.

Astonished, Teela said, "But, you are not a warrior!"

"I am a magician," said Orko. What he did not say was that he knew the great secret of the Masters of the Universe: that Prince Adam was also He-Man, mightiest man in the Universe. He left the surprised Teela and hurried to the prince's tent. Concealed in the prince's baggage was the Sword of Power. Orko wrapped the sword in a blanket. Then, clutching the bundle, he went back to Teela.

"Part of my magician's equipment," said Orko as he mounted Teela's horse behind her. Then, with a shake of the reins, they were off across the plain.

Slipping through the entrance to the Labyrinth Orko unwrapped the Sword. As he floated noiselessly along, the Sword began to glow. And as the glow grew brighter Orko knew that he was getting closer to its owner.

Suddenly there was a loud screech and Orko

almost dropped the Sword. A great hairy orc
jumped in front of him and bared its teeth.
Orko waved his free hand... and there was a
bunch of flowers. The orc stopped, baffled. The
flowers became a goldfish in a bowl, then a
string of flags. Orko threw the flags at the orc,
who became tangled up in them while the little
jester made his escape. A giant centipede rushed
at him. Quick as a flash Orko darted through
the air in a figure of eight, and the surprised
centipede found itself tied in a knot!

The Sword pulsated with light as Orko floated swiftly through the dark tunnels. The gleaming weapon was heavy. It took all of the little alien's strength to keep his grip on it.

He must be almost there, he thought. Then he gulped with horror. A huge shape completely blocked the tunnel. The shape moved, and Orko saw that it was the rear part of a vast animal.

Taking a deep breath, and a firm grip on the Sword with both hands, he swooped on the shape and jabbed hard with the Sword. The creature jumped back, knocking the Sword to the ground and sending Orko somersaulting backwards. He quickly recovered... but where was the Sword? The creature had squeezed round in the narrow passage. The Sword must be somewhere beneath it.

Angry now at having been robbed of the Sword, Orko leapt up to be level with the creature's head and punched its nose hard.

Astonished... no one had ever dared to attack it before... the great beast jumped back a pace. And there was the Sword. Orko dived down, seized the Sword and darted between the enormous legs and along the tunnel.

As Orko appeared panting from between the legs of the behemoth, Prince Adam jumped down from the ledge and took the Sword. With a cry of

"BY THE POWER OF GRAYSKULL!" he became He-Man, mightiest man in the Universe.

As he raised the Sword, the behemoth
retreated in a dazzling blaze of energy bolts. It
roared in panic. And the panic spread to the
other creatures of the Labyrinth.

The passages and tunnels became filled with
stampeding orcs, basilisks and other horrors.

Too late Skeletor and Evil-Lyn heard the
echoing sounds of panic. They were swept off
their feet and left dazed and bruised.

Back on the surface He-Man blasted shut the
entrance to the Labyrinth.

That night, as Prince Adam, he was scolded
by the king for getting lost. He hung his head in
shame... but winked at Orko.

The secret of the Masters of the Universe was
still safe.